Double Trouble

ORCHARD BOOKS
96 Leonard Street, London EC2A 4RH
Orchard Books Australia
14 Mars Road, Lane Cove, NSW 2066
First published in Great Britain 1996
First paperback publication 1997
Text © Lisa Bruce 1996
Illustrations © Lesley Harker 1996
The rights of Lisa Bruce to be identified as the Author
and Lesley Harker as the Illustrator of this Work
have been asserted by them in accordance with the Copyright,
Designs and Patents Act, 1988.
A CIP catalogue record for this book is available
from the British Library.
1 86039 178 8 (hardback)
1 86039 340 3 (paperback)
Printed in Great Britain

Double Trouble

Lisa Bruce

Illustrated by
Lesley Harker

ORCHARD BOOKS

DYNAMITE DEELA

CONTENTS

Chapter One

"Don't do that, Deela," her mother snapped across the kitchen table. "There is no need to shovel your food into your mouth at Formula One speed."

"Sorry, Mum," Deela apologised. "It's just that William is waiting for me."

Deela's sister, Dipali, smirked.

"Deela's got a BOYfriend."

"William and I are partners," Deela retorted quickly. "We do science experiments together, actually."

"What experiments? How to be as messy as possible?" said Dipali, still smirking.

"Of course not. We do proper work," Deela rejoined angrily. "You're so dippy that you wouldn't know an experiment if it hit you in the face."

"Stop arguing you two," said their mother. "I just heard your father arriving. I hope that he has remembered to bring the camping brochures with him."

"Oh, brilliant!" Deela jumped up and down in her seat.

"Oh, Mum do we have to go camping?" Dipali whined. "It will be cold and full of nasty creatures. You know how I hate creatures."

"Hello everybody," their father said. "I've got some after-dinner reading. You girls can help to choose our holiday."

"Can we do it a bit later, Dad?" asked Deela. "It's just that William and I have got an experiment to finish off."

"What kind of experiments have you been doing?" asked her father sitting down.

"Well," said Deela pleased that someone was taking an interest. "We are doing resuscitation and…"

"Oh good," interrupted her mother. "The more people who know how to save lives the better."

Deela frowned. "It's not exactly that..."

But her mother, who was a nurse, went on talking as she cleared the plates away.

"You'd be surprised at the number of cases we get in casualty who could have been saved if somebody knew about life saving. Fetch the ice cream would you please, Dipali."

Dipali trotted out to the large chest freezer while her mother continued lecturing Deela.

"...I am SO glad that you have decided to apply yourself to something worthwhile at last. Tell me what you have been doing."

"Well..." replied Deela slowly, not sure that her mother really wanted to hear.

A shrill scream punctured the air. Deela's mother dropped her spoon in horror and raced towards the freezer.

"Dipali, what's the matter?" she cried.

"That's what we've been doing," Deela muttered.

"Deela," her father groaned. "What have you done?"

Dipali was led back to the table.

"Deela, your sister nearly fainted. Do you know why?" her mother asked angrily.

Deela shrugged. "I guess so."

"Your sister nearly fainted because when she went to get the ice cream there was a mouse on top of it. A large grey mouse."

"And I actually touched it," Dipali shuddered at the thought.

"It wouldn't hurt you," said Deela simply. "It was dead."

Deela's mother glared. "What exactly is a dead mouse doing in my freezer? You'd better have a good explanation, Deela."

"I told you, Mum. We've been doing experiments. With resuscitation. William's cat left it on his doorstep this morning so we put it into the freezer and we are going to bring it back to life."

"Exactly how were you planning to do that?" asked her father sceptically.

Deela sighed. "We were going to attach it to my big torch battery…"

"No, absolutely not," Deela's mother said. "You cannot bring things back to life by passing volts of electricity through them."

"But Frankenstein…"

"That was only a story," Deela's mother folded her arms angrily. "And, it was quite wrong of you to frighten your sister."

Deela was put out.

"We weren't doing it to frighten her. It's not my fault that she's such a scaredy cat."

"That's no excuse, Deela. Tonight, Dipali can help your father to choose our holiday while I teach you how to do real life saving. After you have helped me to clean out the freezer. Mice carry diseases."

"Aw, Mum, that's boring."

"That's enough Deela. Now, go and throw that creature away."

Deela gave the mouse a proper burial at the bottom of the garden. It seemed only fair after the way it had contributed to scientific research. Deela was still cross with her family for not letting her try to revive the little thing. She was sure that it could have gone on to live a long and happy life.

After an hour with her mother learning mouth to mouth resuscitation, Deela had second thoughts. Blowing regular puffs into the mouse's mouth would have been difficult.

"That's right Deela, hold the neck here, tilt the head back." While Deela was practising with one of Dipali's dolls her father and sister walked in.

"Right then," announced Deela's father. "We have chosen a camping site for our holiday. Or rather, Dipali has chosen it."

"Where is it?"

"Hartley Hall," said her father. "The campsite has only just opened in the grounds of the Hall. It's small but the site is beside a lake so there's lots of rowing and sailing available."

"Oh, great!" said Deela excitedly.

"Then there's the Hall itself..."

"That's the only reason I chose it." Dipali could hardly disguise her disgust. "At least we can be indoors SOME of the time."

"...actually it's a stately home which the current Lord Hartley opens to the public during the summer."

"Well," Deela's mother said, glancing over the brochure. "That all sounds fine. I'm sure we'll have a wonderful time."

"A wonderful cold, wet, uncomfortable time," muttered Dipali. "I bet you there won't be a decent clothes shop for miles."

"Of course not," said her father. "Nor will there be a hairdressers. In fact there won't even be a television."

"No television!" Dipali was shocked. "How will I manage?"

"That's simple, you will have the chance to get closer to nature."

Dipali shuddered at the thought. "Living with Deela is as close to nature as I want to get thank you very much."

Chapter Two

Deela, on the other hand, was delighted with the prospect of a fortnight camping in the grounds of Hartley Hall. That is, until she discovered that she was sharing a tent with Dipali.

"Mum," she moaned, "I won't be able to get in our tent if she takes four hair-dryers."

"They are not hair-dryers. This is a hot brush, these are curling tongs and this one has my diffuser."

"What on earth do you want all THAT lot for, Dippy?"

"Well, I have to have something to do at the wretched place."

Their mother sighed and emptied out Dipali's bag onto the bed.

"I think that one hair-dryer and one mirror will be enough dear...and Deela, we are NOT taking your box of stick insects."

"But, Mum, they'll die without me."

"I hardly think so, Deela. You can give them to William to look after. I'm sure that he'll feed them for you and if any of them die, he can practise his mouth to mouth resuscitation."

After much packing, unpacking and repacking Deela and Dipali were ready. The family squeezed all their bags into the back of the car and set off for Hartley Hall.

Chapter Three

The ground where Deela's father was putting up the tents was hard. Not only that, it was about as flat as a cobbled street! He had put up the big tent with the blue and yellow stripes by the edge of the lake and had gone to the site office to pay.

"I'll put the girls' sleeping tent up later," he called as he set off up the field.

Deela was impatient. She wanted her tent to go up straight away.

"I know, I'll get it all set out for him," she

said, but her mother was too busy to listen.

"No, Dipali, you won't freeze in the night if you sleep on the ground… Yes, I will make sure that there isn't a single daddy long legs in the tent when you go to bed…"

Deela set to work. She shook all the bits and pieces out of the bag. They jangled to the ground in a clatter of pegs and poles. It looked easy. First Deela spread out the canvas, then she fitted the poles together to make a frame. Next came the tricky bit. She had to get the poles inside. Deela undid the zip and wormed her way in, dragging the poles behind her. CLANG! They all fell apart and Deela had to crawl around fitting

them back together again. She got very hot and sweaty under the clinging green canvas.

"Done it!" she cried as the last pole slotted into place. It had worked. Deela felt very proud of herself. In no time at all the tent was up.

"Deela," called her father. "I was going to help you with that."

"It's all right, Dad. I've managed to do it by myself."

Deela's father looked at the tent. It stood on wobbly poles, leaning heavily to the left with guy ropes spreading out in every direction like a drunken spider. He went over and shook the top. To his surprise the tent stayed up.

"Well done, Deela," he said. "It may need a little straightening, but apart from that it seems fine."

"Dad," interrupted Dipali urgently. "Where's the loo?"

Their father pointed to a small hut on the far side of the field. "It's over there."

Deela and Dipali raced over the long grass and Deela reached the door first. It was wooden with several slats missing and from behind it came an unmistakable odour. Dipali took one look inside at the rows of cubicles.

"Ugh!" she shrieked. "I can't go in there. Anyone can see in!"

"I guess you haven't got much choice," said Deela. "You'll use anything if you're desperate enough."

"No, no, no," insisted Dipali. "I refuse to go in. It's smelly, it's not private and I will die, I know I will."

"Don't be so silly, Dippy."

With a sudden lurch Deela pushed against her sister sending her flying into the toilet. Dipali was furious but very much alive.

"I'll get you for this, Deela! You wait!"

Dipali didn't have to wait long. That afternoon their father announced that he had tickets for them to go on a tour around the stately home.

Chapter Four

Hartley Hall was huge. Its four turrets stretched up to pointed tips high in the sky. Row upon row of windows stared blankly out over ornamental gardens and the fields beyond. In the distance was the woodland and the lake where the family was camping.

"Fancy actually living here," said Deela as they climbed the last flight of steps to the carved double doors.

"It must have been wonderful," sighed her sister. "Just imagine sweeping up the drive in a carriage and having a butler waiting to open the door for you."

"Lord Hartley still lives here," their father said.

"Lucky thing," Dipali muttered.

Their footsteps echoed in the long wood panelled hallway. Dark figures in old oil paintings gazed down at them from their lofty perches and everywhere smelt of beeswax and dust. Deela ran up and down the curling staircase until her father hissed at her to stop.

"I bet that you could have some brilliant games of hide and seek here," she said.

"Don't you dare," warned her mother. "This furniture is very expensive."

"At least it's civilised here," said Dipali staring enviously at a tall four-poster bed in Lady Amanda's bedroom.

"Why is that curtain moving?" Deela asked.

"Which curtain?" said her mother.

"That one, over by the mirror."

"That's a tapestry wall hanging, not a curtain," explained her mother glancing up from the guide book. "It was sewn by the Lady Amanda Hartley while her husband was away fighting."

"That doesn't explain why it was moving," said Deela.

"Maybe it was the wind," said her mother moving on to look at Lady Amanda's bathroom.

Deela shrugged but she wasn't convinced. The air in the room hung in motionless boredom. There was no breeze to have moved the material.

From behind the rich velvet curtains came a muffled sound. Deela cocked her head to one side.

"What's that noise?"

"I can't hear anything," said Dipali haughtily from where she was studying her reflection in an ornate mirror.

"Shh, listen. I think I can hear someone crying." Deela frowned. "It's coming from over by the curtain."

Dipali smirked. She had a brilliant idea.

"Why don't you have a look," she said. She knew Deela would get into trouble but it would pay her back for the toilet trick.

Deela had to investigate. She climbed over the red twisted rope that separated the visitors from the antique furniture and instantly a loud alarm clanged. Before Deela had even reached the bed an angry looking attendant appeared.

"What's going on?" cried the attendant.

"Come out of there this instant," called Deela's father.

"I'm so sorry," said Deela's mother trying to calm the attendant down. "She won't do it again."

"Deela you are leaving right now," said her father, sternly. "You can't come back until you learn to behave yourself."

Deela didn't really mind. She had seen enough marble fireplaces and suits of armour for one holiday. Something about the Hall bothered her. For some reason she couldn't shake off the feeling that she was being watched. She wanted to get down to the lake and to explore the woods.

Chapter Five

The water on the lake was a soft inky blue. It looked sparklingly cool and refreshing. Tall trees crowded the edges of the lake bending their branches over to touch the delicious water. Everything was peaceful in the warm afternoon sunshine. In the soothing sun the two girls changed into their swimming costumes and plunged into the inviting water. They had such good fun that Dipali even forgot about her dislike of camping for a while.

"Hey, Deela, over here!"

SPLASH!

"Watch it, Dippy!"

"Serves you right."

"Can't catch me," Deela swam away fast
and found herself facing the shore.

"Dipali, look over there," she called, "by the jetty."

"What is it?"

"Can you see someone, moving about in the bushes?"

"No," said Dipali scornfully.

"I think that someone is watching us."

Suddenly Dipali thought of another way of getting her own back on her sister.

"Oh yes," she cried excitedly, "I saw something move, too."

Swimming next to Deela, Dipali whispered in theatrical voice, "You don't think it is the Hartley Ghost, do you?"

"The what?"

"Didn't you listen to the guide in the Hall? Apparently there is a phantom who stalks the grounds wailing and moaning…"

"Shut up, Dippy." Deela splashed her sister. "I don't believe you."

Deela swam away then stopped and called back over her shoulder, "And I don't believe in ghosts either, so there."

Deela sounded confident but as she scanned the shoreline Deela was sure that she saw the bushes move again. She didn't believe in ghosts, but there was something suspicious about the movement on the lakeside. Something which made Deela's neck tingle. For some reason she couldn't shake off the feeling that all was not well.

Chapter Six

That night the air smelt sweet under the thin canvas of the tent. Deela could hear the gentle lapping of the water against the jetty. She was having difficulty in sleeping. For one thing the ground under her sleeping bag was bumpy and it was very difficult for her to get comfortable. For another thing, she needed to go to the loo.

It was no good, Deela decided that she had to get up. She climbed carefully out of her sleeping bag so as not to wake the sleeping Dipali and edged her way out of

43

the tent. Slipping on her wellingtons Deela
set off across the field. The campsite looked
strange and eerie in the moonlight. The
other tents in the field rustled gently like
great sleeping dinosaurs.

The toilet block was silent and in the hushed moonlight Deela felt as though she was the only living person around. It was creepy and Deela didn't want to stay out too long. Quickly she walked back through the dew soaked grass and was about to unzip the tent when she heard a rustle in the trees beside her. She stopped. Deela looked towards the noise. Shadows flitted eerily but no one came out.

A shiver charged up Deela's spine. It must be the ghost! Deela froze. For once in her life she didn't know what to do. Her normally active voice had deserted her and Deela found that she couldn't squeak let alone scream. Then, HORRORS! A silver-grey figure appeared at the edge of the trees. Deela saw it glide silently through the shadows towards her.

In that instant Deela found her voice. "Help!" she screamed. The figure floated towards her. Deela instinctively took a step backwards…and tripped over a guy rope.

The little tent decided that enough was enough. It couldn't stay up any longer. With a swoosh the canvas flopped down on top of Dipali who had woken up at the sound of Deela's scream. Sleepily she batted the canvas off her face, not understanding what was going on. Material flapped crazily as she tried to get out.

With a huge effort Dipali stood up wrenching the last of the tent pegs out of the ground. Staggering, she lurched forwards, broken tent poles clanging together and guy ropes dangling. It was a terrible sight. Deela's father poked his head out of the big tent.

"What's going on?" he mumbled.

"Get me out of here," came a muffled voice from inside the collapsed tent as Dipali staggered blindly around the field.

Deela picked herself up in time to see the ghost floating backwards onto the jetty. Dipali was getting nearer and nearer.

"Come back, Dippy!" Deela shouted but it was too late. Dipali and the tent reached the edge of the jetty then veered away wildly with a clatter of poles and pegs. The ghost stepped backwards. With hardly a splish, it slid under the shiny black water.

Suddenly there was a furious splashing and gurgling sound. The ghost was shouting for help. Deela stood up and raced out to the end of the jetty. The ghost wasn't a ghost at all. It was a boy!

"Aaaargh!" cried the boy as his head disappeared under the water. The surface of the lake rippled as though a large object underneath was struggling but the boy didn't reappear.

Chapter Seven

Without wasting a moment, Deela did the first thing that came into her head. She threw off her wellingtons and dived into the lake. The water was so cold that for a moment it took Deela's breath away. Even with her eyes open it was so dark under the water that Deela couldn't see a thing.

She was just about to surface for another gulp of air when she felt a hand touch her leg. Deela reached out for the body. It was limp and lifeless. Deela groped under the boy's armpits and hauled him with her up to the surface.

By then Deela's father had reached the end of the jetty. He leant down and grasped the heavy weight from Deela's hands.

"Quick," he gasped. "Let's get him out." With a heave, Deela's father pulled the dripping body onto the wooden jetty. Deela climbed up, water streaming off her like a waterfall.

Deela looked down at a small still face, pale in the moonlight and surrounded by spikes of blonde hair. She hadn't seen anything that looked more like a drowned rat in her life.

"That's why I thought that he was a ghost," said Deela staring at the boy's feet. "He's wearing rollerboots." Deela looked anxiously at her father.

"Who is he, Dad?"

"He's in trouble," said her father, "who ever he is. He's not breathing. Let's get your mother, she'll know what to do."

"No, Dad," said Deela urgently. "There's no time. I can do it," Deela pushed her father to one side and quickly slipped her finger into the boy's mouth to check that it wasn't blocked.

"You call Mum, I'll start."

Deela tipped back the boy's head just like her mother had told her and, clamping her mouth over the pale lips, Deela blew in gently. It must have only taken three puffs before Deela felt a movement. The boy coughed and splurted water from his lungs.

By then Deela's mother, who had been untangling Dipali, came over and took charge.

"There, there," she soothed putting the boy into the recovery position. "Everything is all right."

Deela's father and Dipali brought towels and blankets to wrap Deela and the boy in.

"Who are you?" asked Deela curiously. The boy rubbed his wet face and hair with a towel.

"My name is Felix. Lord Hartley is my grandfather."

"What are you doing out here at this time of night?"

"I was running away."

"Running away! From Hartley Hall!" Dipali was shocked. She couldn't imagine anyone wanting to leave such luxury.

Felix began to shake. Deela's mother put her arm around him to help him stand up.

"Let's go to the tent," she suggested. "I'll make everyone a nice hot cup of tea."

Chapter Eight

Dried and dressed, the children sipped their milky tea gratefully.

"Now then," said Deela's mother, calmly, "maybe Felix would like to tell us why he was running away."

Felix gulped. "My parents are abroad and they've left me with Grandfather. He's so old that he never goes anywhere and I'm not allowed out by myself. The fields and the woods and the lake look so inviting that I decided to leave. I'd much rather be outside than in that stuffy old Hall."

"Quite right," nodded Deela who couldn't imagine spending all her time indoors, even if it was a big house.

"I took my rollerboots so that I could escape quickly and I was just putting them on when Deela came out of the toilets. She frightened me. The rest you already know."

"But really, Felix," said Deela's mother gently, "your grandfather will be worried about you. Look what happened to you."

Felix looked downcast.

"I'm sorry," he said. "Will you tell him that I'm sorry."

"You will be able to tell him yourself. Deela's father has gone to wake him up."

"Why did you go straight to the bottom of the lake when you fell in?" Deela asked Felix. "You really gave me a fright."

"I can't swim," Felix answered simply.

"Really!" It was Deela's turn to be surprised. Swimming to her was as natural as walking. "Would you like me to teach you?"

Felix's eyes shone in the torch light.

"Oh thank you, that would be brilliant."

"You can have your first lesson tomorrow."

For the first time that night Felix smiled.

Just then, Deela's father came back with Lord Hartley.

"What have you been doing, Felix?" asked Lord Hartley looking concerned.

Deela nudged Felix, "People are always asking ME that!" Felix smiled.

"I've been making friends, Grandad. Deela is going to teach me how to swim and do you know something?"

Lord Hartley smiled. "What?"

"I think that I *am* going to enjoy the holidays here," said Felix smiling back at his grandfather.

Deela grinned from ear to ear.

"So do I," she said happily.